APR 17 2018

W9-ADI-045

Barbie™

Bedtime Story Collection

Published in the United States by Random House Children's Books, a division of Random House LLC, 1745 Broadway, New York, NY 10019, and in Canada by Random House of Canada Limited, Toronto, Penguin Random House Companies. The stories contained in this work were originally published separately by Random House Children's Books as follows: *Barbie™ Mariposa & The Fairy Princess: True Fairy Friends,* in 2013, adapted by Mary Man-Kong and illustrated by Ulkutay Design Group, based on the original screenplay by Elise Allen; *Barbie™ in The Pink Shoes: In the Spotlight,* in 2013, adapted by Mary Man-Kong and illustrated by Ulkutay Design Group, based on the original screenplay by Alison Taylor; *Barbie™ The Princess & The Popstar: Best Friends Rock!,* in 2012, adapted by Mary Man-Kong and illustrated by Ulkutay Design Group, based on the original screenplay by Steve Granat & Cydne Clark; *Barbie™ in A Mermaid Tale,* in 2010, adapted by Mary Man-Kong and illustrated by Ulkutay Design Group and Pat Pakula, based on the original screenplay by Elise Allen; *Barbie™ in A Mermaid Tale 2: A Fairy-Tail Adventure,* in 2012, adapted by Mary Man-Kong and illustrated by Ulkutay Design Group, based on the original screenplay by Elise Allen; *Barbie™ Princess Charm School,* in 2011, adapted by Mary Man-Kong and illustrated by Ulkutay Design Group, based on the original screenplay by Elise Allen; *Barbie™ A Fairy Secret,* in 2011, adapted by Mary Man-Kong and illustrated by Ulkutay Design Group, based on the original screenplay by Elise Allen; *Barbie™ A Fashion Fairytale,* in 2010, adapted by Mary Man-Kong and illustrated by Dynamo Limited, based on the original screenplay by Elise Allen; *Barbie™ and The Three Musketeers,* in 2009, adapted by Mary Man-Kong and illustrated by Ulkutay Design Group and Allan Choi, based on the original screenplay by Amy Wolfram; *Barbie™ Thumbelina,* in 2009, adapted by Mary Man-Kong and illustrated by Ulkutay Design Group and Allan Choi, based on the original screenplay by Elise Allen; *Barbie™ Mariposa,* in 2008, adapted by Mary Man-Kong and illustrated by Rainmaker Entertainment, based on the original screenplay by Elise Allen; *Barbie™ & The Diamond Castle,* in 2008, adapted by Mary Man-Kong and illustrated by Ulkutay Design Group and Allan Choi, based on the screenplay by Cliff Ruby & Elana Lesser; *Barbie™ as The Island Princess,* in 2007, adapted by Mary Man-Kong, based on the original screenplay by Cliff Ruby & Elana Lesser; and *Barbie™ in The Twelve Dancing Princesses,* in 2006, adapted by Mary Man-Kong, based on the original screenplay by Cliff Ruby & Elana Lesser.

randomhouse.com/kids

Educators and librarians, for a variety of teaching tools, visit RHTeachersLibrarians.com

ISBN 978-0-385-38784-2

MANUFACTURED IN CHINA

10 9 8 7 6 5 4 3 2 1

Barbie™

Bedtime Story Collection

Random House 🏠 New York

Contents

Barbie™ Mariposa & The Fairy Princess: True Fairy Friends • 7

Adapted by Mary Man-Kong • Illustrated by Ulkutay Design Group
Based on the original screenplay by Elise Allen

Barbie™ in The Pink Shoes: In the Spotlight • 29

Adapted by Mary Man-Kong • Illustrated by Ulkutay Design Group
Based on the original screenplay by Alison Taylor

Barbie™ The Princess & The Popstar: Best Friends Rock! • 51

Adapted by Mary Man-Kong • Illustrated by Ulkutay Design Group
Based on the original screenplay by Steve Granat & Cydne Clark

Barbie™ in A Mermaid Tale • 73

Adapted by Mary Man-Kong • Illustrated by Ulkutay Design Group and Pat Pakula
Based on the original screenplay by Elise Allen

Barbie™ in A Mermaid Tale 2: A Fairy-Tail Adventure • 95

Adapted by Mary Man-Kong • Illustrated by Ulkutay Design Group
Based on the original screenplay by Elise Allen

Barbie™ Princess Charm School • 117

Adapted by Mary Man-Kong • Illustrated by Ulkutay Design Group
Based on the original screenplay by Elise Allen

Barbie™ A Fairy Secret • 139

Adapted by Mary Man-Kong • Illustrated by Ulkutay Design Group
Based on the original screenplay by Elise Allen

Barbie™ A Fashion Fairytale • 161

Adapted by Mary Man-Kong • Illustrated by Dynamo Limited
Based on the original screenplay by Elise Allen

Barbie™ and The Three Musketeers • 183

Adapted by Mary Man-Kong • Illustrated by Ulkutay Design Group and Allan Choi
Based on the original screenplay by Amy Wolfram

Barbie™ Thumbelina • 205

Adapted by Mary Man-Kong • Illustrated by Ulkutay Design Group and Allan Choi
Based on the original screenplay by Elise Allen

Barbie™ Mariposa • 227

Adapted by Mary Man-Kong • Illustrated by Rainmaker Entertainment
Based on the original screenplay by Elise Allen

Barbie™ & The Diamond Castle • 249

Adapted by Mary Man-Kong • Illustrated by Rainmaker Entertainment
Based on the original screenplay by Cliff Ruby & Elana Lesser

Barbie™ as The Island Princess • 273

Adapted by Mary Man-Kong
Based on the original screenplay by Cliff Ruby & Elana Lesser

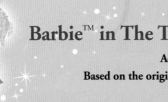

Barbie™ in The Twelve Dancing Princesses • 297

Adapted by Mary Man-Kong
Based on the original screenplay by Cliff Ruby & Elana Lesser

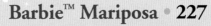

Barbie
Mariposa
& the
Fairy Princess

True Fairy Friends

$\mathcal{M}$ariposa was a beautiful Butterfly Fairy who lived in the magical kingdom of Flutterfield. Everyone adored Mariposa. She loved to read books and knew more about fairy history than anyone else.

One day, Queen Marabella gave Mariposa a special assignment—to travel to Shimmervale and restore friendship with the Crystal Fairies.

The Crystal Fairies believed that long ago, the Butterfly Fairies tried to steal some of their Crystallites—the life force of their kingdom.

Mariposa knew the stories were untrue, but she was still nervous about meeting the Crystal Fairies.

Mariposa was amazed when she reached Shimmervale.
A fairy named Talayla met her, but all the other fairies were
afraid of the Butterfly Fairy.

When Mariposa and her pet puffball, Zee,
arrived in Shimmervale, they were led into the royal
throne room, where they met King Regellius and
Princess Catania.

Mariposa was amazed by all the beautiful Crystallites and
reached out to touch one.

"Don't touch that!" barked the distrustful king.

Startled, Mariposa bumped into the king with her wings,
making everything worse!

Princess Catania wanted Mariposa to feel welcome, so she took her visitor on a tour of Shimmervale. Catania led the way on her flying horse, Sylvie. At the magical Glow Water Falls, the two fairies happily skipped Rainbow Rocks. They quickly became good friends.

Princess Catania told
Mariposa a secret. Long ago,
an evil fairy called Gwyllion
had asked for a Crystallite, but
King Regellius refused. Gwyllion
was so angry that she captured Catania and
dropped her from high in the sky. Catania fell
to the ground and never flew again. Since then,
King Regellius didn't trust fairies from outside
Shimmervale.

But Catania trusted Mariposa. "This Crystallite is for you," she said, giving Mariposa a sparkling crystal necklace.

"I have something for you, too," Mariposa said as she handed Catania a gorgeous glowing Flutterfield Flutter Flower.

"I love it!" exclaimed the princess. "Thank you."

The two fairy friends hurried back to the castle—they had to get ready for the Crystal Fairy Ball! Mariposa and Catania were soon dazzling and shimmering in their beautiful gowns. Mariposa folded down her big butterfly wings to keep them out of the way.

"If you're going to fold your wings, so will I," Catania said.

At the Crystal Fairy Ball, the two friends had a great time laughing and dancing—until Mariposa's Crystallite necklace fell to the floor.

"Mariposa, you stole a Crystallite!" accused the king. "After we welcomed you and trusted you!"

Catania tried to explain, but King Regellius wouldn't listen.

"Leave!" he shouted at Mariposa. "Immediately!"

As Mariposa and Zee sadly flew back toward Flutterfield, they noticed a strange-looking fairy flying toward Shimmervale. Mariposa immediately realized that it was Gwyllion from Catania's story!

Mariposa knew she had to warn the Crystal Fairies, so she quickly flew back to Shimmervale.

When she arrived, all the Crystal Fairies were already frozen under Gwyllion's spell! Mariposa asked Catania for help, but the princess was too scared.

"I can't fly!" cried Catania.

23

There was no time to waste, so Mariposa flew after Gwyllion alone. The evil fairy was preparing to destroy the Heartstone, the biggest Crystallite in Shimmervale. If she succeeded, Shimmervale would freeze forever!

"Gwyllion, stop!" Mariposa shouted.

"No more interruptions!" the evil fairy cackled as she blasted Mariposa with her magic staff.

Suddenly, with a burst of courage, Catania flew up to help Mariposa. The princess snapped Gwyllion's magic staff in two, breaking the evil fairy's wicked spells. "Catania!" Mariposa cried happily. She was thrilled that the princess could fly! "You made it!"

"Not fast enough," said Catania. "Look!"

The Heartstone was shaking, shuddering, and turning cold and dark!

Just then, Mariposa noticed something glowing in Catania's pocket. "The Flutter Flower!" exclaimed Mariposa. "Hold it close to the Heartstone!"

The enchanted Crystallite began to glow. It burst into a colorful rainbow of beautiful bright lights. Shimmervale was saved!

"Your wings!" Mariposa and Catania exclaimed at once, pointing at each other. Their wings and outfits were now sparkling with beautiful crystals!

"I owe you an apology,"
King Regellius said to Mariposa.
"I misjudged you. I was wrong."
Then the king turned to punish
Gwyllion, but Catania stopped him.
The princess gave her own Crystallite
necklace to Gwyllion.
"I'm righting a wrong," Catania said to Gwyllion. Catania
knew that by being a friend, she would be making one, too.
Gwyllion was touched by the gift and promised to live
up to Catania's trust in her.

27

That evening, there was a huge celebration for the two kingdoms of Shimmervale and Flutterfield. The Butterfly Fairies and the Crystal Fairies danced the night away. They would be true fairy friends forever!

Barbie™ in The Pink Shoes

In the Spotlight

It was the day of the big ballet recital and everyone was excited—especially Kristyn. The young dancer loved all the spins, jumps, and twirls in all the famous ballets.

Kristyn watched the star ballerina, Tara, rehearse. She wished that she could dance the lead role.

When it was Kristyn's turn to dance, she glided and twirled beautifully on the stage—and then she started to add some of her own dance moves.

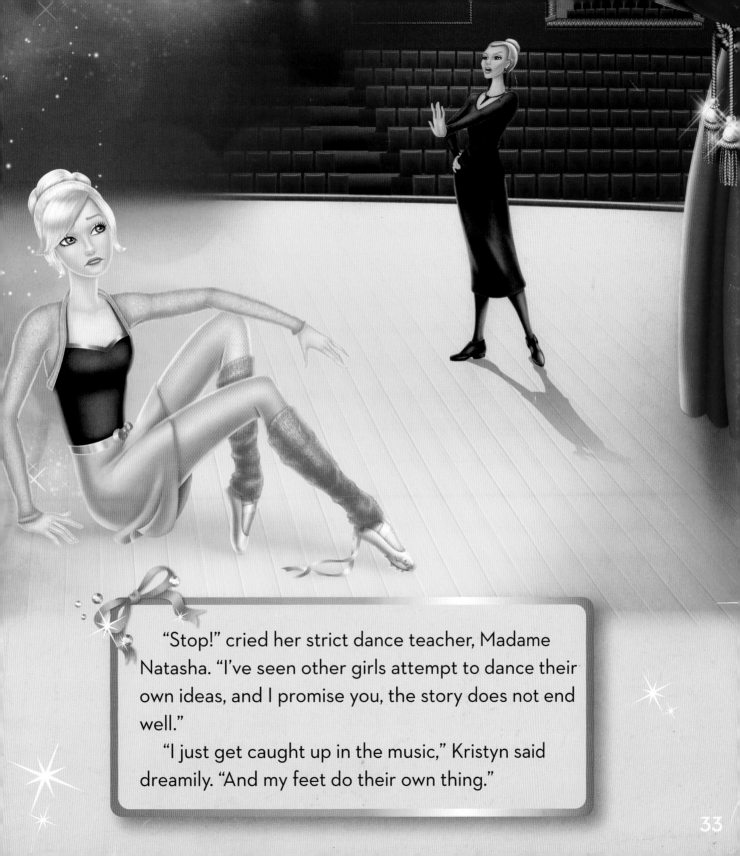

"Stop!" cried her strict dance teacher, Madame Natasha. "I've seen other girls attempt to dance their own ideas, and I promise you, the story does not end well."

"I just get caught up in the music," Kristyn said dreamily. "And my feet do their own thing."

33

After rehearsal, Kristyn noticed that her ballet shoe was ripped. She went with her best friend, Hailey, to see the costume designer, Madame Katerina. Hailey was Madame Katerina's assistant.

Madame Katerina searched everywhere. She handed
Kristyn a pair of pink shoes. "These are for you, my dear,"
she said.

Kristyn sat down and slowly laced up the pink ballet shoes. As she stood up, the shoes began to glitter and sparkle. Magically, Kristyn's dress transformed into a beautiful blue-and-pink tutu and her hair turned strawberry blond. The costume shop had disappeared— and Kristyn and Hailey found themselves in a strange forest. They were amazed!

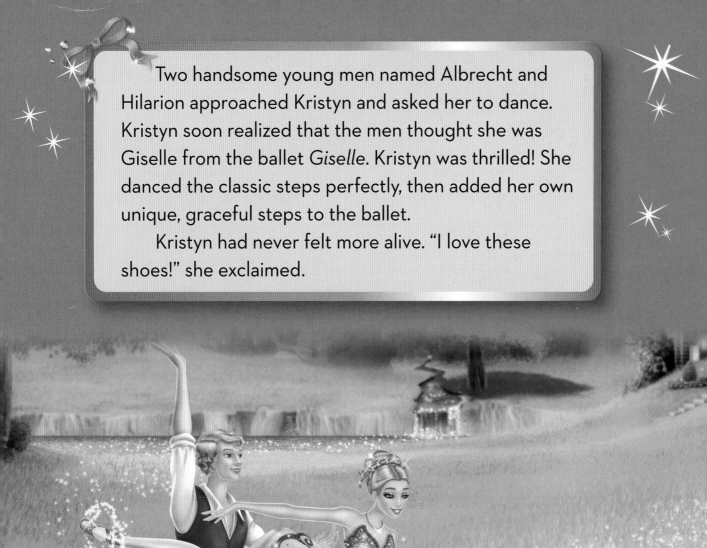

Two handsome young men named Albrecht and Hilarion approached Kristyn and asked her to dance. Kristyn soon realized that the men thought she was Giselle from the ballet *Giselle*. Kristyn was thrilled! She danced the classic steps perfectly, then added her own unique, graceful steps to the ballet.

Kristyn had never felt more alive. "I love these shoes!" she exclaimed.

After the dance, Hilarion and Albrecht started to argue about who should marry Giselle. Not wanting any trouble, Hailey quickly pulled Kristyn into the forest.

Suddenly, a grand ice sleigh appeared. "What is happening here?" the evil Snow Queen demanded. "I will not tolerate this kind of disruption. The ballet must be perfect. Bring the girl to me!"

As the girls ran through the forest, Hailey realized what was happening. "It must be the shoes," said Hailey. "When you put them on, we ended up in the middle of the ballet. But if you take them off . . ."

"No way," said Kristyn. She had never been the star ballerina before this.

Just then, Kristyn's hair turned a rich chestnut brown and her dress transformed into a gorgeous purple gown. A group of ballet dancers appeared and placed a glittering swan crown on her head. Kristyn had become the Swan Queen Odette in the ballet *Swan Lake*!

A handsome young prince named Siegfried appeared and asked Kristyn to dance. As they performed a beautiful duet, the prince couldn't take his eyes off Kristyn.

"I know we've just met," said the prince, "but I want to invite you to a party tonight at my royal pavilion." Kristyn graciously accepted.

After the prince left, the girls noticed a man in a dark cloak approaching. They quickly recognized him as the evil magician Rothbart from *Swan Lake*. Rothbart wanted the prince to marry his daughter Odile, so he magically made her look like Odette. Then he cast an evil spell on Kristyn and Hailey—transforming them into swans! Every day when the sun set, they would change back into humans. But when the sun rose, the girls would change back into swans!

Kristyn knew from the ballet that the only way to break the spell was to make the prince fall in love with her. She and Hailey flew as fast as they could to reach the palace at sunset.

When the prince saw Odile and Kristyn, he didn't know who the real Odette was. Kristyn had an idea. She started to dance, and the prince recognized her graceful, unique moves. He chose Kristyn and the spell was broken!

Unfortunately, the Snow Queen had witnessed the change in the *Swan Lake* ballet—and kidnapped Hailey!

Kristyn quickly raced to the Queen's palace, where she found Hailey frozen in a block of ice. The evil Snow Queen cast a spell on Kristyn, controlling every move she made. But Kristyn closed her eyes and concentrated. She began to spin and dance in her own beautiful style.

"Stop that!" cried the Queen. "There is only one way to tell the story."

"No," Kristyn replied. "There is more than one way."

As she uttered those words, rays of light shone through the palace. The spell was broken—and the Snow Queen disappeared forever.

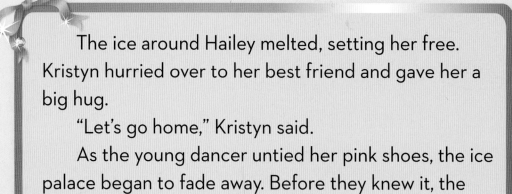

The ice around Hailey melted, setting her free. Kristyn hurried over to her best friend and gave her a big hug.

"Let's go home," Kristyn said.

As the young dancer untied her pink shoes, the ice palace began to fade away. Before they knew it, the two friends were safely back at their ballet school.

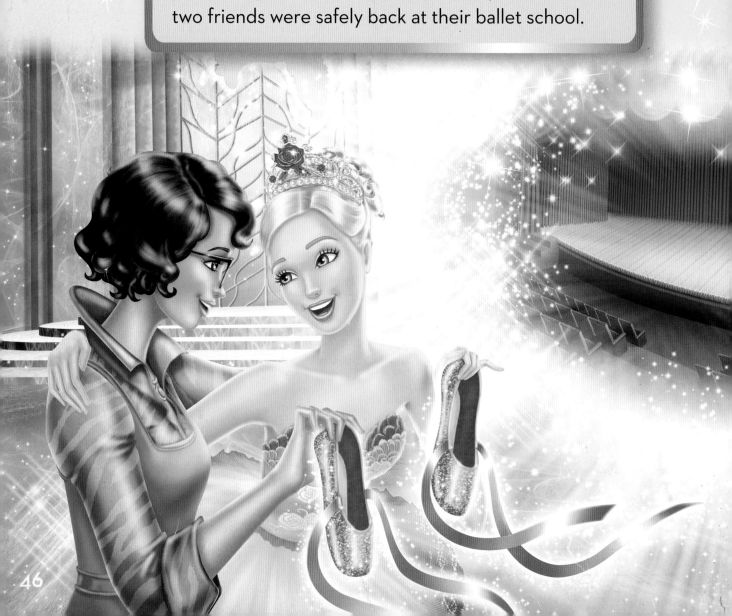

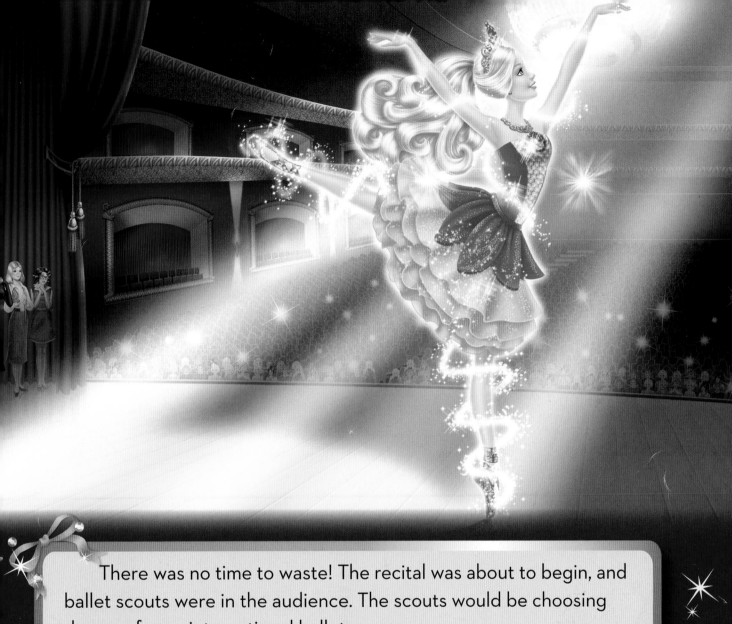

There was no time to waste! The recital was about to begin, and ballet scouts were in the audience. The scouts would be choosing dancers for an international ballet company.

When it was Kristyn's turn to dance, she glided onto the stage. The music seemed to flow into Kristyn, and she performed her own unique dance moves with all her heart. As she twirled, her dress transformed into a pink gown and her hair flowed beautifully behind her. Everyone was amazed! Even Madame Katerina nodded approvingly as Kristyn danced.

47

After the recital, the ballet scouts chose Tara to star in their production of Giselle. But they also chose Kristyn and her original dance style as the inspiration for a new ballet.

Kristyn and Hailey were so happy. Kristyn had followed her heart and her ballet dreams had come true.

Far away in the kingdom of Meribella, the beautiful Princess Tori greeted visitors for the country's five hundredth anniversary celebration. Tori loved being a princess. But after curtsying all day long, she wished she could trade her boring royal duties for the fun and exciting life of a pop star.

Meanwhile, the pretty pop star Keira was singing at a concert for her adoring fans. Keira enjoyed being a pop star, but she wished she could trade her busy life of shows and tours for the carefree and pampered life of a princess.

Princess Tori was so excited when Keira arrived in Meribella to perform at the anniversary celebration—the princess was Keira's biggest fan!

When the girls met at the palace, Tori let Keira try on her tiara.

"I've got just the outfit to go with it!" Keira said as she waved her magical microphone. Instantly, the pop star's clothes transformed into the gorgeous gown Princess Tori was wearing.

Tori pulled out her magical hairbrush and waved it around her head. Her prim and proper curls transformed into a wild punk-rock hairdo! Then the girls waved the hairbrush and microphone at each other.

"You look like me!" both girls exclaimed.

Disguised as each other, the girls went on a tour of the palace.

The princess led Keira down an ancient staircase to a secret garden.

The pop star was amazed to see flying garden fairies! They were protecting a plant that glittered with diamonds.

"That's the Diamond Gardenia," Tori explained. "Without it, our kingdom would wither and die."

The garden fairies took two diamond seeds that had fallen on the ground and made a star necklace for Keira and a heart necklace for Tori.

"We'll wear them as friendship necklaces so we'll always remember today," Tori told Keira.

Princess Tori spent the morning practicing Keira's dance routine. She loved singing and dancing onstage. Tori knew the steps so well that none of the choreographers suspected she wasn't really Keira!

After breakfast, Keira, now in her princess best, took the royal carriage to a flower show. No one could tell she wasn't really Princess Tori!

Tori was having so much fun pretending to be Keira! It gave her a great idea. "Why can't we keep on being each other?" she asked. "It'd be magical!"

The girls agreed to switch places for a day.

The next day, Tori had the time of her life pretending to be a pop star. But while practicing some difficult dance moves, she tripped and fell!

Keira was enjoying her day as a princess. But when she put her feet up on the royal dining table, the pop star got locked in Tori's bedroom for bad manners and unprincess-like behavior!

Tori didn't know that Keira was locked away, and she was beginning to panic! Keira's concert was about to start, and Tori was terrified at the thought of singing in front of the whole kingdom. But when she realized that Keira was counting on her, the princess took a deep breath, walked onstage, and sang beautifully. The crowd cheered!

While everyone was at the concert, Keira's greedy manager, Crider, and his assistant sneaked into the secret garden. After tearing the Diamond Gardenia from its roots and scooping up all the diamonds, they made their getaway in the royal carriage.

Luckily, Keira had escaped from the locked bedroom. She ran into Tori, and the two girls raced after Crider.

As the carriage sped away, Tori and Keira looked up at an overhead lantern cable. Realizing that Crider's carriage would be passing beneath it in just moments, the two friends grabbed hold of the cable.

"Three, two, one!" Tori counted. She and Keira used the cable as a zip line.

"I think that belongs to my kingdom," Tori declared as they stopped Crider and recovered the Diamond Gardenia.

The girls hurried back to the palace and tried to replant the Diamond Gardenia, but it was too late. Suddenly, Tori remembered their friendship necklaces. "We have the seeds!" Tori exclaimed.

The girls quickly planted the diamonds—and two new Diamond Gardenia plants sprouted!

With Meribella saved, Keira and Tori raced back to the concert.

Looking like herself again, Keira walked onto the stage. "Please welcome my best friend—Her Royal Highness Princess Tori!" she announced. The crowd went wild, and the two girls hugged each other tightly.

The princess and the pop star sang a beautiful duet. Keira realized that although she had enjoyed playing a princess, she really loved being a pop star. And Tori realized that although it was fun living like a pop star, she really loved being a princess.

Tori and Keira had learned that they could always count on each other—and that best friends rock!

Barbie in A Mermaid Tale

A storybook

Merliah Summers smiled as she rode the waves.
Ever since she was a little girl, Merliah had been
able to swim like a fish. Now she was one of the best
surfers in Malibu.

As Merliah surfed, she thought everything was perfect—until she noticed her hair. It was *turning bright pink*!

Shocked and embarrassed, Merliah wiped out and dove below the waves. To her amazement, she found that she could *breathe underwater!*

"Merliah?" someone said. A sparkly pink dolphin was talking to her! "My name is Zuma. I am a friend of your mother, Calissa. She is the mermaid queen of Oceana— but she needs your help."

Merliah couldn't believe that her mother was a magical mermaid—and that she was half mermaid herself! Merliah learned that when she was a baby, her mother's wicked sister, Eris, had taken over Oceana. The fortune-telling Destinies had foretold that Merliah would one day defeat Eris. So to protect her baby daughter, Calissa had sent Merliah to live with her human grandfather in Malibu.

As they swam toward a cove, Zuma explained that long ago, Calissa's wicked sister, Eris, had taken over Oceana. To protect her daughter, Calissa had given Merliah a special shell necklace.

Merliah didn't want to believe she was half mermaid! She ripped off her necklace and smashed it against the rocks. Suddenly, Merliah saw a vision of her mother being held prisoner.

Merliah just wanted her hair—and her life—back the way it was. *Maybe my mother's magic can help me return to normal,* Merliah thought. So she agreed to help.

With Zuma as her guide, Merliah journeyed underwater to the most gorgeous place she had ever seen! Oceana was bustling with colorful fish and fashionable merfolk.

"Amazing!" Merliah exclaimed.

"We'll have to disguise your legs," Zuma told Merliah. She didn't want anyone to know that the young surfer was in Oceana—especially not Eris.

Zuma quickly brought Merliah to the boutique run by her friends Xylie and Kayla.

"Tail makeover!" Xylie and Kayla exclaimed.

At the palace, Eris snuck down to the secret dungeon where Calissa was locked away. The evil mermaid had learned that Merliah was in Oceana.

"Tell me where she is," Eris snarled at Calissa.

But Calissa refused to answer.

Meanwhile, the Destinies had told Merliah how to stop Eris. She needed to complete three important tasks.

The first task was to find the Celestial Comb, hidden in the Yafos Caves. No mermaid could climb the steep rock wall to reach the comb. But Merliah had legs, and she scaled the wall quickly. "I've got it!" she cried triumphantly.

The second task was to impress a dreamfish so that it would grant her a wish. Zuma knew exactly where the dreamfish could be found: in the Adenato Current. The powerful swirling water was impossible to swim in—but Merliah could surf it! The dreamfish were amazed.

"Call when you need me, and I will come," promised one young dreamfish.

The third task was the hardest. Merliah needed the necklace that Eris always wore around her neck. Merliah knew that Eris would appear at her daily festival, so she came up with a plan. Merliah, Xylie, and Kayla starting singing to distract Eris.

"You're the queen of the waves!" sang the friends.

As Eris watched the show delightedly, Merliah
snuck up behind her—and snatched the necklace!

"Stop her!" Eris cried.

The evil mermaid's manta sharks swam after Merliah and ripped off her fake tail!

"You!" Eris cried, realizing that Merliah was Calissa's daughter. Eris quickly captured the young surfer in a powerful whirlpool.

Merliah called for the dreamfish. He appeared and offered to return her to her normal life in Malibu. Merliah was tempted. But her mother and Oceana needed her, so she decided to stay and help.

Suddenly, Merliah's legs magically
transformed into a sparkly *real* mermaid tail.
Merliah couldn't believe it!

"I am Merliah, half-mermaid princess of Oceana,"
she cried proudly, and leapt out of the whirlpool.
"And it is my duty to protect my subjects."

"Get her!" Eris ordered her guards.

"You don't need to listen to her," Merliah said. "I am the rightful heir to the throne. I have the Celestial Comb!"

Enraged, Eris tried to push Merliah back into the whirlpool. But Merliah quickly swam out of the way. The wicked mermaid was sucked into the powerful swirling water and transported to the deepest, darkest trench in the ocean.

The crowd cheered. Eris was gone forever!

Calissa was overjoyed to see her daughter. She wanted Merliah to stay in Oceana. Merliah was happy, too—but she missed her human life in Malibu. Calissa hugged Merliah and placed a magical necklace around her neck. Whenever she wished on the necklace, Merliah could transform from human to mermaid—and back again. "Then you can move easily between the human world and the underwater world," Calissa said.

Merliah was thrilled that she would have a home in both worlds!

Merliah Summers couldn't have been happier. She had just won the big Malibu surfing competition—which meant she would soon be going to the World Championship Surf Invitational in Australia!

"You were lucky, mate," sneered Kylie Morgan, Merliah's biggest rival. "But your luck's gonna run out down under— that's *my* turf."

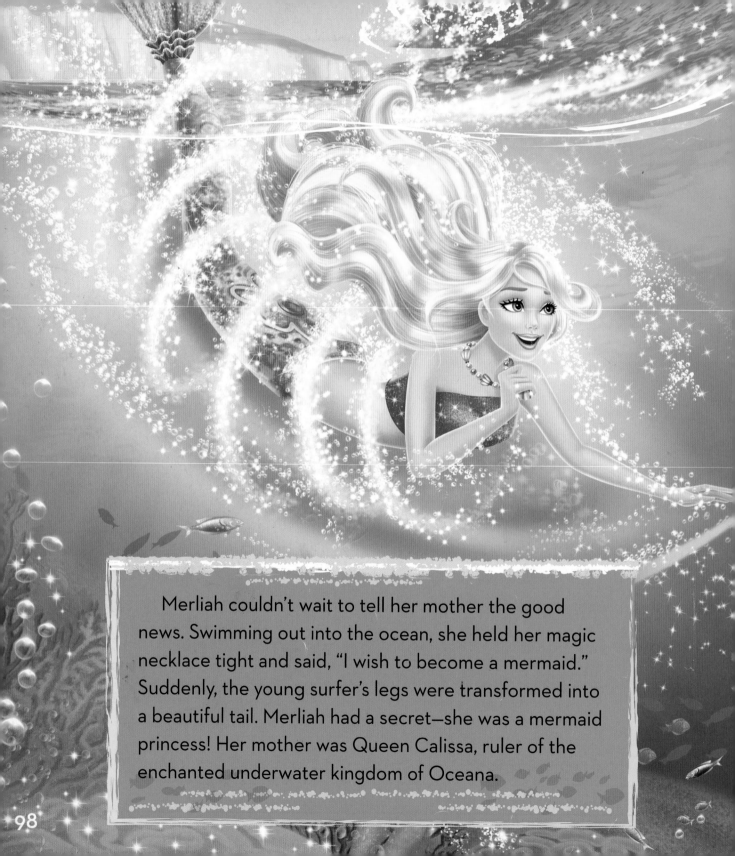

Merliah couldn't wait to tell her mother the good news. Swimming out into the ocean, she held her magic necklace tight and said, "I wish to become a mermaid." Suddenly, the young surfer's legs were transformed into a beautiful tail. Merliah had a secret—she was a mermaid princess! Her mother was Queen Calissa, ruler of the enchanted underwater kingdom of Oceana.

After congratulating her daughter for winning the surfing competition, the queen invited Merliah to the very important Changing of the Tides ceremony. Every twenty years, a member of the royal family sat on the ancient throne to regain the power to make Merillia, the life force of the ocean.

Merliah couldn't participate in the Changing of the Tides ceremony. If she did, she would lose forever her ability to change back into a human. But Calissa thought it was Merliah's duty to at least attend the ceremony. Unfortunately, it was on the same day as the surfing competition, and Merliah was determined to be there instead. The queen was very disappointed.

Kylie won the first round of the World Championship Surf Invitational, but Merliah received all the attention from the reporters and fans. She had performed a handstand on her board during her run!

"But I won!" Kylie exclaimed angrily.

As Kylie fumed on the beach, a talking rainbow fish named Alistair appeared beside her. Alistair told Kylie that the secret to Merliah's success was her magic necklace.

So Kylie stole the necklace and used it to turn into a mermaid. Then Alistair promised to take Kylie to someone who could teach her the secrets of surfing.

Alistair led Kylie down to the bottom of the ocean. Suddenly, the fish pushed the young surfer into a whirlpool! Kylie became trapped and Queen Calissa's evil sister, Eris, was released. Months before, Eris had been imprisoned in the whirlpool for trying to take over Oceana. Now free, the wicked mermaid was going to try again, at the Changing of the Tides ceremony!

Luckily, Merliah's sea lion friend, Snouts, saw what had happened to Kylie. Swimming as fast as he could, Snouts found Merliah and led her to the whirlpool. Together, they rescued Kylie.

"I never should have taken your necklace," Kylie said. "And if your aunt is going to hurt the ocean, I want to help stop her."

Meanwhile, as she was preparing tea for the Changing of the Tides ceremony, Calissa heard a chilling voice. "You're not setting a place for me?" Eris asked.

The evil mermaid cast a spell on her sister, and Calissa's worst nightmare came true—her tail turned to stone! Helpless, the queen sank to the ocean floor.

When they learned that Queen Calissa was in danger, Merliah and Kylie rushed to help. But the queen's tail was too heavy. They could not carry her to the Changing of the Tides ceremony!

"The only way to stop Eris from taking over Oceana is if I sit on the throne," said Merliah.

"But if you do that, you'll lose your legs forever," Calissa warned.

"I am the princess of Oceana," Merliah said. "It's my duty. And it's my choice."

Merliah and Kylie raced to the Changing of the Tides
ceremony and knocked Eris off the throne. Merliah sat on
the throne, but when the magical lights of the Changing
of Tides shone down on her, nothing happened.

"You have no tail!" Eris said, cackling. "You can't activate the throne!"

Realizing what she had to do, Kylie took a deep breath. She quickly took the magic necklace from her own neck and put it around Merliah's.

"I wish to become a mermaid," Merliah declared. Suddenly, her legs transformed into a glorious mermaid's tail and the throne was bathed in colorful glowing lights. Merliah had stopped Eris—and gained the power to make Merillia! Oceana was saved!

"Nooo!" Eris cried. She tried to cast a nightmare spell on Merliah, but the spell bounced off the throne and hit Eris instead. The evil mermaid's worst nightmare came true—she had human legs!

With the spell broken, Calissa's tail turned
back to normal. She swam back to the throne
and hugged Merliah.

Merliah was happy to have saved Oceana, but she was sad that she could no longer surf. As she and her mother swam back to the surface with Kylie, magical light swirled around her—and her tail turned back into legs!

"The ceremony must have transformed you into your truest self," Calissa explained. "You are both a mermaid *and* a human."

"Now you can surf in the meet!" exclaimed Kylie. "Come on!"

Later, as the two friends rode the waves, Merliah forgot all about the competition. She was too busy creating glistening Merillia. "I'm loving this!"

Kylie won the competition, and Merliah was very happy for her. But more importantly, Merliah realized how lucky she was to have good friends and family, above and below the sea.

In a small apartment on the outskirts of the town of Gardania, a beautiful young girl named Blair Willows lived with her foster mother and her little sister, Emily.

Blair was excited—she had won the lottery to attend Princess Charm School, the most prestigious school in Gardania!

At Princess Charm School, girls were trained to become princesses and Lady Royals, trusted princess advisors. Blair knew her life as a hardworking waitress was about to change forever.

"Welcome to Princess Charm School!" Madame Privet told Blair. "Everyone here has princess potential." She handed Blair a school uniform and assigned her a sprite named Grace.

Then Blair met Isla and Hadley, two friendly princesses-in-training who were her new roommates.

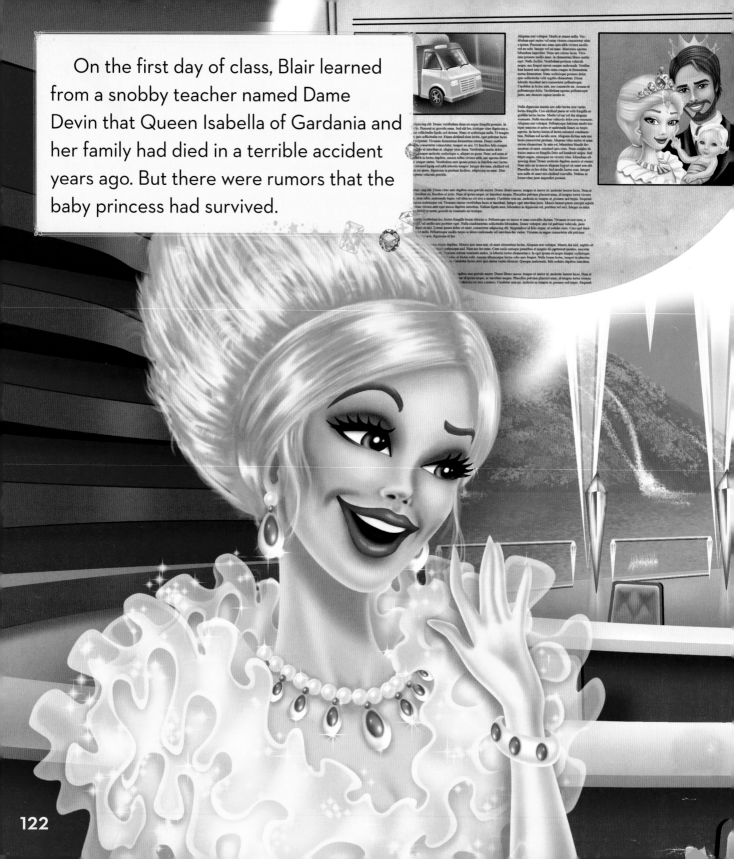

On the first day of class, Blair learned from a snobby teacher named Dame Devin that Queen Isabella of Gardania and her family had died in a terrible accident years ago. But there were rumors that the baby princess had survived.

If the true heir was not found, Dame Devin's daughter, Delancey, was next in line for the throne.

Dame Devin didn't like Blair—or any other students— stealing the spotlight from her daughter.

Delancey and her mother did their best
to get rid of Blair.

But with the help of her friends, Blair worked
hard for many weeks. Soon she outshone
Delancey in all their classes.

Dame Devin was furious. She secretly had Blair's, Isla's, and Hadley's uniforms destroyed. According to the Princess Charm School rules, students who didn't attend classes in uniform were expelled!

When the girls discovered their uniforms ripped to shreds, they didn't know what to do. "Coronation Day is only two days away and we'll be expelled!" Hadley exclaimed.

"I have an idea," Blair declared confidently.

Soon Blair and her friends were sewing the tattered pieces into stylish outfits.

Minutes later, the three friends raced to their etiquette class. "Those aren't school-issued uniforms!" Dame Devin cried.

"They are made from our original uniforms," Blair said. "We've just used some hard work to unlock our princess potential."

Dame Devin fumed. She wanted to get Blair thrown out of Princess Charm School—fast.

The next day, Blair, Hadley, and Isla discovered a portrait of Queen Isabella as a young woman. The queen looked just like Blair!

"You must be her daughter, Princess Sophia!" Hadley cried.

"You're the rightful heir to the throne, not Delancey," said Isla.

From her hiding place in the shadows, Delancey also saw the resemblance and was shocked.

Blair, Hadley, and Isla returned to their room to find Dame Devin waiting for them. The teacher had secretly hidden her jewels in the girls' room and accused the girls of stealing.

"Lock them up!" Dame Devin cried to the guards.

Luckily, Delancey released the three friends. She knew Blair was the true heir to the throne and wanted to help her. Delancey gave the girls a map of the palace and told them where Gardania's Magical Crown could be found. The crown would reveal the truth: it only glowed when it was worn by the true heir of Gardania!

Blair, Hadley, and Isla quickly followed the map to a secret vault—and found Gardania's Magical Crown.

Suddenly, Dame Devin appeared and snatched the crown from its pedestal. "You'll never be more than a poor lottery girl," she cried to Blair.

Dame Devin slammed the door and reset the password on the keypad. The girls were locked in the vault!

133

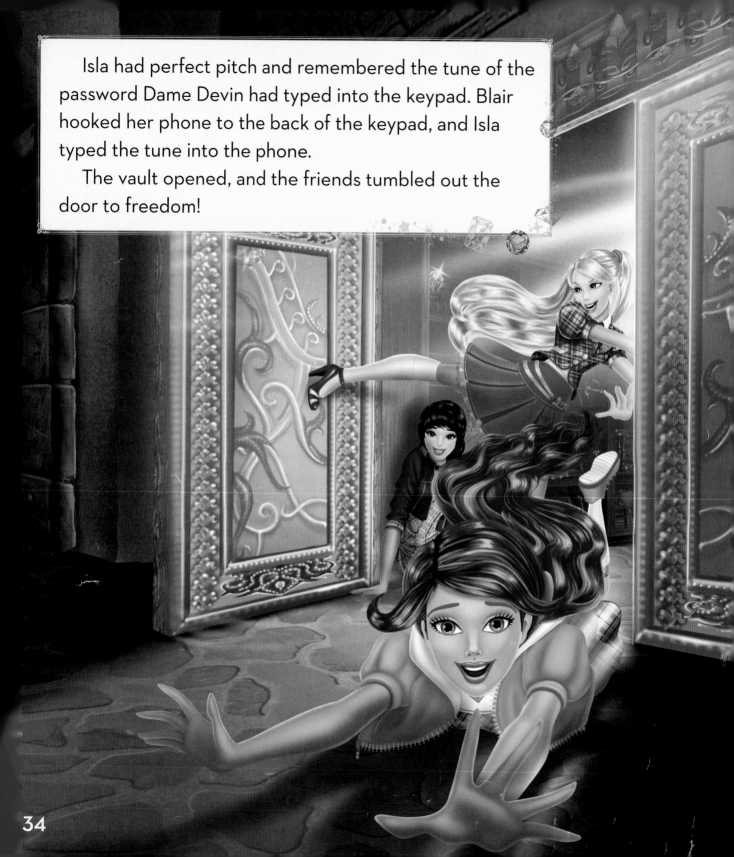

Isla had perfect pitch and remembered the tune of the password Dame Devin had typed into the keypad. Blair hooked her phone to the back of the keypad, and Isla typed the tune into the phone.

The vault opened, and the friends tumbled out the door to freedom!

Blair and her friends raced through the palace and burst into the palace ballroom.

"I am Princess Sophia, daughter of Queen Isabella!" Blair declared.

Dame Devin tried to grab Gardania's Magical Crown, but Grace and the other fairy assistants were too quick. They whisked the crown away and placed it on Blair's head.

The crown magically glowed brighter and brighter, and Blair's outfit transformed into a beautiful royal gown.

"It is Princess Sophia!" the crowd gasped.

"No!" cried Dame Devin as she was taken away.

Blair was thrilled to be crowned Princess of Gardania. "I promise to always work hard and live up to my princess potential," she said.

To thank her for all her help, Blair asked Delancey to be her Lady Royal.

"I would be honored . . . Your Highness," Delancey said with a smile.

The friends hugged each other and went into the palace to celebrate. They knew that in every girl was a princess with dreams that sparkled brightly.

It was the premiere of Barbie's latest movie. Everyone was excited and happy—except for Raquelle, Barbie's costar. Angry that Barbie was getting all the attention, Raquelle had a wicked idea. She stepped on Barbie's gown—and ripped it!

Carrie and Taylor, Barbie's stylists, sprang into action. They fixed Barbie's gown by magic—fairy magic, that is. No one knew that Carrie and Taylor were fairies from a beautiful fairy world called Gloss Angeles.

The ruler of Gloss Angeles was Princess Graciella.
Everyone adored the princess—except for Crystal, her royal
attendant. Crystal was in love with Graciella's boyfriend,
Zane, and wanted to steal him away. So Crystal gave Graciella
a magic potion that made her forget about Zane and fall
in love with Barbie's boyfriend, Ken.

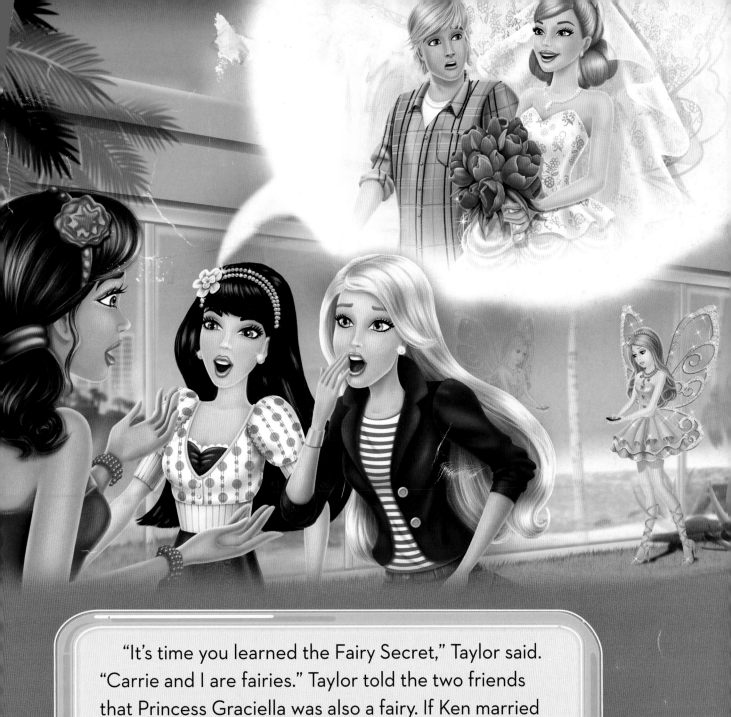

"It's time you learned the Fairy Secret," Taylor said. "Carrie and I are fairies." Taylor told the two friends that Princess Graciella was also a fairy. If Ken married her, he would have to stay in Gloss Angeles forever. "We've got to save him!" cried Barbie.

Carrie and Taylor brought Barbie and Raquelle to Lilianna Roxelle. "She's the oldest and wisest fairy living in the human world," explained Carrie.

Lilianna believed that the princess was under a love spell and gave Barbie a magical mist to break it.

Then Lilianna showed them a secret passage to the fairy world. . . .

"It's incredible!" Barbie exclaimed. "I can't believe it's real."

Barbie and Raquelle quickly bought beautiful clip-on wings.

They tried to fly, but a huge gust of wind knocked them down.

Luckily, they were caught by some winged ponies.

"You're a good rider," Barbie said to Raquelle. "I know you can get us to the palace."

The girls rushed into the royal palace and tried to rescue Ken. Graciella was furious! "Freeze!" the princess cried, and she trapped Barbie and Raquelle in a fairy cage. Then the princess used her magic to make Ken propose to her. Soon they would be married—and Ken would be trapped in the fairy world!

Barbie and Raquelle tried to escape from the fairy cage, but the bars were too strong.

"I'm sorry I've been so mean to you," Raquelle said to Barbie. "Can you forgive me? Do you think we can be friends?"

"We *are* friends," Barbie said as she gave Raquelle a big hug.

Their forgiveness was so powerful that suddenly, the fairy cage disappeared and the girls' clip-on wings transformed into beautiful *real* wings.

155

Using their new wings, the two friends flew as fast as they could to stop the wedding. Princess Graciella threw sparkling balls of light at them, but Barbie and Raquelle were too fast.

Barbie flew overhead and sprinkled magical mist on Graciella—and the spell was broken! The princess immediately remembered that she loved Zane, not Ken.

Zane proposed to Princess Graciella, and she happily said yes. The couple decided to get married on the spot— with Barbie, Raquelle, Carrie, and Taylor as their bridesmaids.

Princess Graciella realized that Crystal had given her the love potion, so she gave her attendant a fitting punishment: Crystal had to clean up after the royal wedding reception!

"Thank you for breaking the spell," Graciella told the three friends. "You are always welcome to come back to Gloss Angeles."

"Wait until we tell people about this place!" said Raquelle.

But Princess Graciella cast a spell on Barbie, Ken, and Raquelle. They would believe that their time in the fairy world was all a dream—and Gloss Angeles would remain a fairy secret.

159

Back in the human world, Carrie and Taylor said goodbye to Barbie, Raquelle, and Ken. They had to return to Gloss Angeles.

"I had the strangest dream about being in a fairy world last night," Raquelle told Barbie. "And I woke up feeling like we're friends."

"I had the same dream," Barbie replied with a smile. "But I *know* we are friends—good friends."

Barbie™
A Fashion Fairytale

$\mathcal{L}$ook!" Barbie exclaimed to her pet poodle, Sequin. "Paris!" Barbie was so excited. She was flying to France to visit her aunt Millicent at her famous fashion house.

When Barbie arrived at Millicent's, she was greeted with a warm hug. But Aunt Millicent had some bad news. "I'm closing my fashion house and moving to the country."

Aunt Millicent's assistant, Alice, told Barbie why Millicent's was closing. A mean designer named Jacqueline and her assistant, Delphine, had stolen all Millicent's fashion ideas and sold them as their own. Now no one wanted Millicent's designs. A short time later, Millicent closed her shop.

Millicent was heartbroken. She had to decided to sell the building to a company called Hot Dogeteria.

165

Barbie was sad. "When I was younger, I used to think Millicent's was a magical place," Barbie confided to Alice.

"I think it still is," said Alice. "Legend has it that magical creatures could be summoned from inside this antique wardrobe to help fashion designers."

The two girls quickly placed a dress that Alice had designed inside the wardrobe and closed the doors.

Suddenly, the wardrobe was filled with sparkling lights. Then three Flairies flew out.

"We are Glimmer, Shimmer, and Shyne," said the Flairies. "We give flair to fashions we love!"

Barbie and Alice looked in the wardrobe. Alice's dress glittered and sparkled. It was fabulous!

Barbie had an idea. If she and Alice held a fashion show and sold lots of dresses, they could save Millicent's!

Barbie and Alice cut and sewed beautiful new outfits all night. And the Flairies used their magical powers to make each new design glimmer, shimmer, and shine.

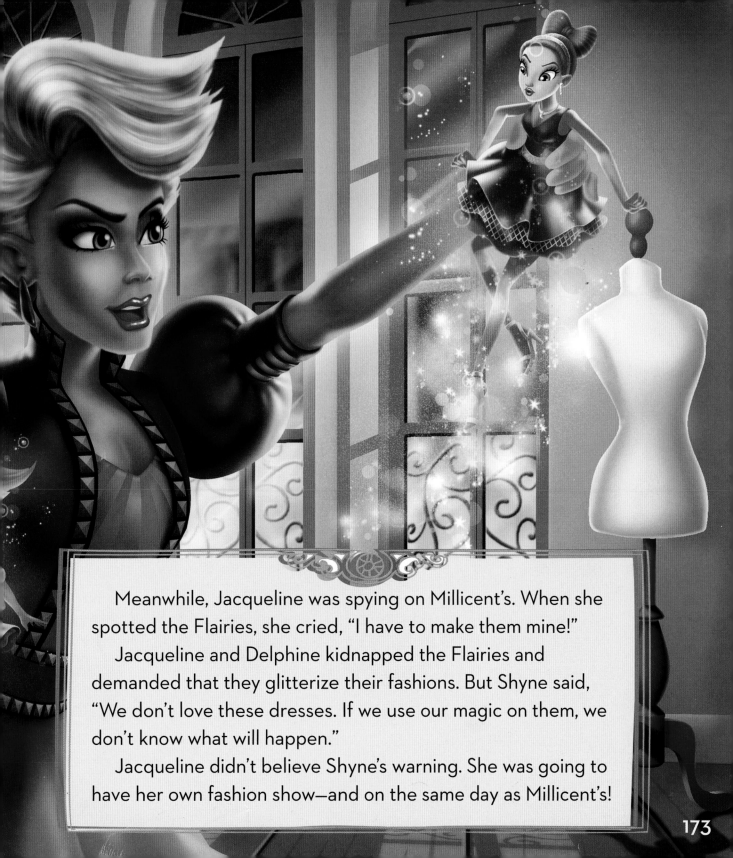

Meanwhile, Jacqueline was spying on Millicent's. When she spotted the Flairies, she cried, "I have to make them mine!"

Jacqueline and Delphine kidnapped the Flairies and demanded that they glitterize their fashions. But Shyne said, "We don't love these dresses. If we use our magic on them, we don't know what will happen."

Jacqueline didn't believe Shyne's warning. She was going to have her own fashion show—and on the same day as Millicent's!

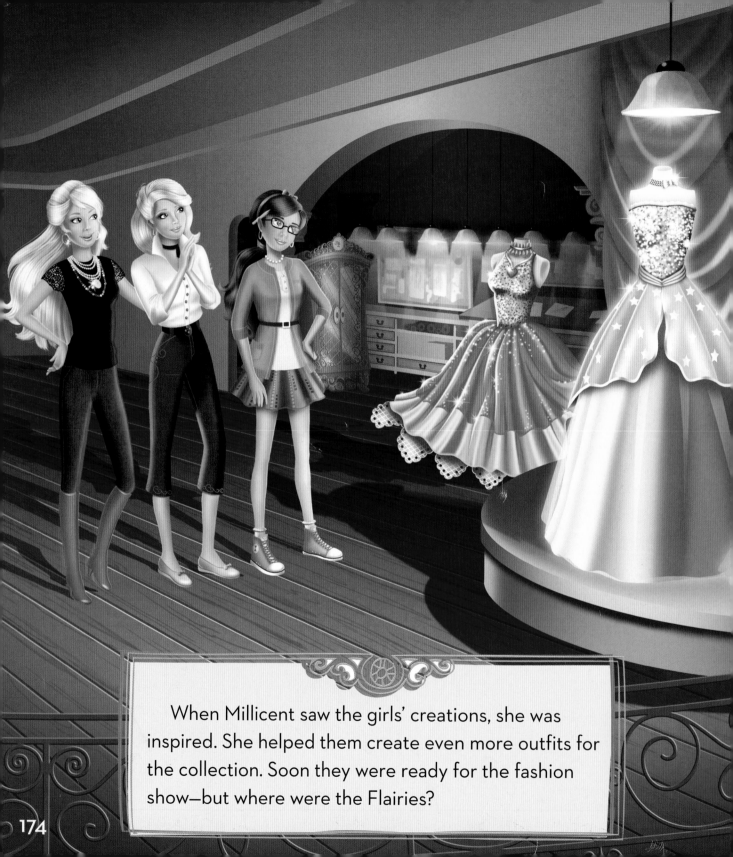

When Millicent saw the girls' creations, she was inspired. She helped them create even more outfits for the collection. Soon they were ready for the fashion show—but where were the Flairies?

That night, as everyone slept, Sequin awoke to bright sparkling lights coming from Jacqueline's. It was the Flairies! They were using their magic to light up the store window and get the pets' attention.

Sequin and her new animal friends quickly rescued Glimmer, Shimmer, and Shyne from the mean designer's fashion house.

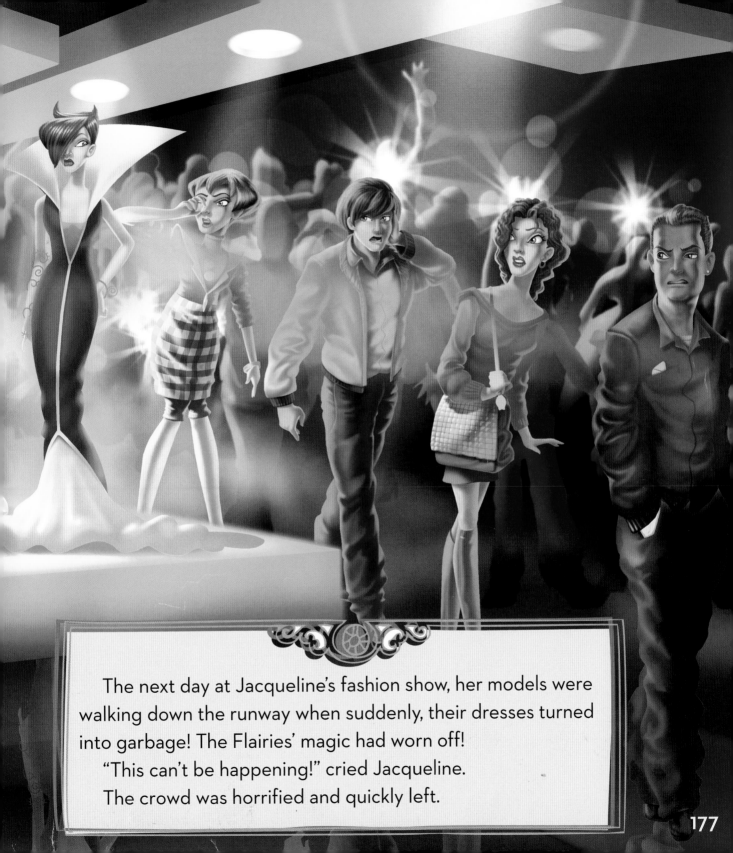

The next day at Jacqueline's fashion show, her models were walking down the runway when suddenly, their dresses turned into garbage! The Flairies' magic had worn off!

"This can't be happening!" cried Jacqueline.

The crowd was horrified and quickly left.

At Millicent's, Barbie and Alice were relieved that the Flairies had returned safe and sound. But Alice was nervous. What if the audience didn't like their outfits?

"We put our heart and soul into these designs," Barbie said. "Now let's rock this party!"

Barbie walked down the runway wearing the creations from Millicent's fashion house. After each spectacular design, the crowd burst into applause. And as Barbie modeled the final outfit, the Flairies added a little extra glimmer, shimmer, and shine. Everyone cheered!

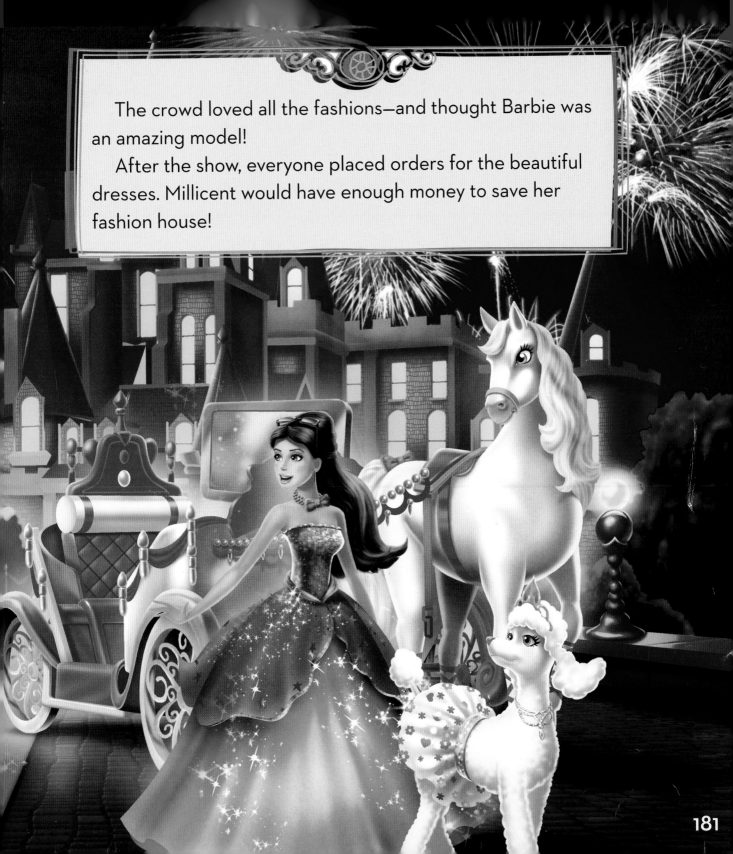

The crowd loved all the fashions—and thought Barbie was an amazing model!

After the show, everyone placed orders for the beautiful dresses. Millicent would have enough money to save her fashion house!

"We did it!" Barbie said to Alice and Millicent. "We believed in ourselves, and the audience loved us!"

"Magic happens when you believe in yourself," said Alice and they watched the Flairies away into the night.

Barbie™ and The
Three Musketeers

In a small village in France, there lived a beautiful girl named Corinne who loved to fence. Corinne dreamed of one day becoming a Musketeer and protecting the royal family in the city of Paris.

When she arrived in Paris, Corinne met with Monsieur Treville, the head of the Musketeers.

"I want to be a Musketeer," Corinne said. "Please give me a chance."

Unfortunately, she was told that she did not have enough experience and training. Corinne was heartbroken!

With no other choice, Corinne gratefully accepted the royal
housekeeper's offer to become a maid in the castle. Everyone
was busy preparing for a special masquerade ball for Prince
Louis. He would become king in a few days.

But the prince's royal advisor, Philippe, had other
ideas. Philippe believed that *he* should be king, so he
came up with a plan to get rid of Louis.

As Prince Louis walked through the castle's great
hall, one of Philippe's men sent the chandelier crashing
down—narrowly missing the prince!

Then the ceiling started to collapse! Corinne and three
other maids, named Viveca, Renée, and Aramina, quickly
sprang into action. They smashed, cracked, shattered, and
broke all the falling pieces. Thanks to them, no one was hurt.

"Where did you learn to move like that?" asked Renée.

"Ever since I was a little girl, I've dreamed of being a Musketeer," Corinne said.

"So have we!" said the other maids.

Every day, the four friends secretly practiced. They wanted to prove to everyone that they could be Musketeers.

The day before the masquerade ball, Corinne noticed men sneaking swords into the castle. She tried to warn the guards that the prince's life was in danger, but they didn't believe her. To make matters worse, Philippe ordered Corinne and her friends to leave the castle—and never return!

The girls would not give up, so they came up with a plan
to save Prince Louis.

"All for one and one for all!" Corinne, Viveca, Renée, and
Aramina cried together.

Viveca designed four costumes. Then Aramina
taught everyone how to dance, and Renée sketched
a map of the castle.

"We can do this!" said Corinne.

The night of the masquerade ball, Corinne, Viveca, Renée, and Aramina disguised themselves in gorgeous gowns. No one recognized them as they entered the castle.

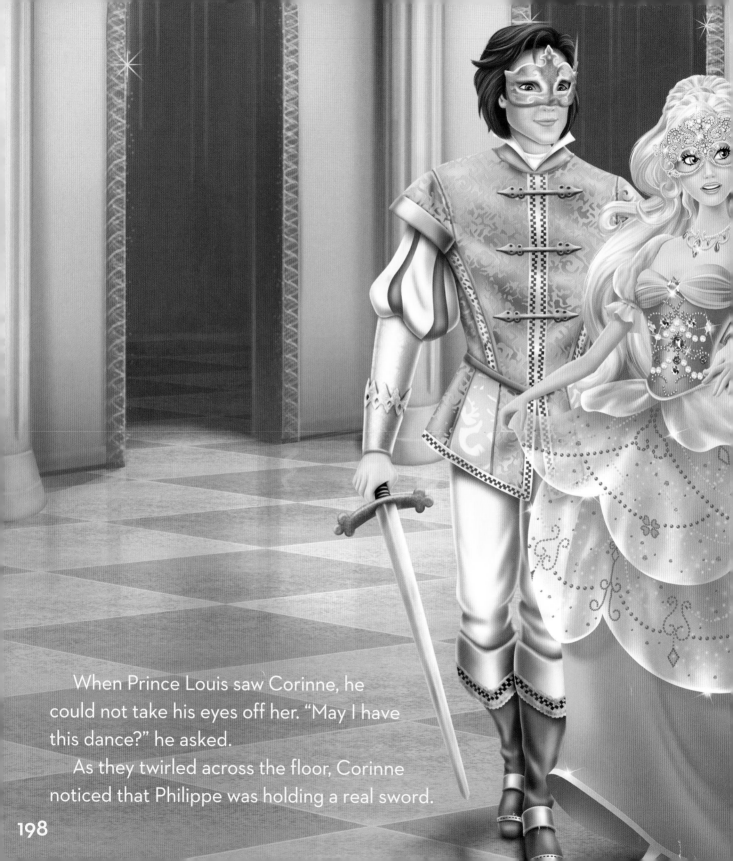

When Prince Louis saw Corinne, he could not take his eyes off her. "May I have this dance?" he asked.

As they twirled across the floor, Corinne noticed that Philippe was holding a real sword.

Suddenly, Philippe and his men surrounded Louis.
But the girls were ready!
"Prepare for battle!" Corinne shouted.

The four friends quickly used their swords, ribbons, fans, and bow and arrow to stop Philippe's men.

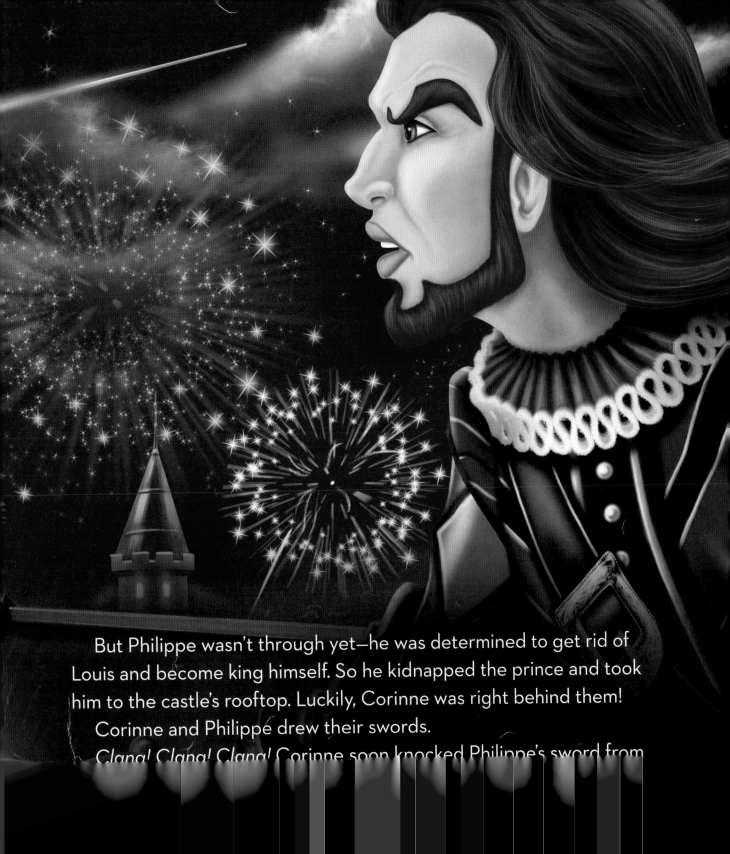

But Philippe wasn't through yet—he was determined to get rid of Louis and become king himself. So he kidnapped the prince and took him to the castle's rooftop. Luckily, Corinne was right behind them! Corinne and Philippe drew their swords.

Clang! Clang! Clang! Corinne soon knocked Philippe's sword from

Corinne, Renée, Aramina, and Viveca had proved that they were brave, so the prince declared them Musketeers.

"All for one and one for all!" the four friends cried.

Barbie™ Thumbelina

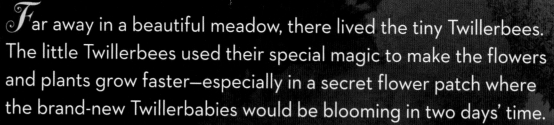

Far away in a beautiful meadow, there lived the tiny Twillerbees. The little Twillerbees used their special magic to make the flowers and plants grow faster—especially in a secret flower patch where the brand-new Twillerbabies would be blooming in two days' time.

The Twillerbees were very shy and always stayed hidden—except for Thumbelina. She was the bravest Twillerbee of them all.

"I'm flying!" exclaimed Thumbelina as she soared in the air with colorful flower-petal wings she had made for herself and her friends. "But Twillerbees can't fly," said Janessa. "It's just not possible."

"Anything is possible if you truly believe you can do it," Thumbelina said.

Rumble! Rumble! Suddenly, the girls saw giant machines approaching.

"Humans!" Janessa cried. "We should go, right now!"

But it was too late! The flower patch beneath them was lifted out of the ground by one of the machines. Thumbelina, Chrysella, and Janessa were trapped!

They discovered that a spoiled human girl named Makena
had had their flower patch transported to her home to impress
a snooty girl named Violet. And Makena's parents were going
to build a skateboard factory right on Twillerbee Field!

The three Twillerbees soon found themselves inside
a fabulous apartment where humans lived.

Thumbelina was mad. "Who do you think you are?" she said as she confronted Makena.

"What are you?" Makena asked as she tried to catch the tiny Twillerbee.

Luckily, Thumbelina and her friends quickly escaped out a window. "We have to do something!" Thumbelina told her friends. They had to save Twillerbee Field.

"We're way too small to make any difference in what they do," Janessa said.

"We're small," said Thumbelina. "But that doesn't mean we're helpless."

With the help of Lola the hummingbird, Thumbelina's friends flew back to Twillerbee Field to warn the others. Then Thumbelina headed to Makena's apartment to try to stop the humans from destroying their home.

Back inside, Thumbelina tried to persuade Makena to save Twillerbee Field. "If you convince your parents to stop building their factory, I'll make special things for you." Thumbelina used her magic and quickly wove some leaves from a bush to create a beautiful purse. "But you mustn't tell anyone about me."

Makena promised. But she really wanted to impress Violet. So Makena secretly invited Violet to see the fabulous new purse— and Thumbelina.

That afternoon, Janessa, Chrysella, and all the other Twillerbees went to work. Using their special magic, they spun leafy vines through the engines, wheels, motors, and levers of all the humans' construction equipment. Twillerbee Field was saved—if only for a little while.

216

The next morning, Thumbelina surprised Makena by magically transforming her wilting plants into beautiful flowers. Touched, Makena tried to convince her parents to stop construction on the skateboard factory. Unfortunately, they were too busy to listen.

Makena promised to try again, but first she had to get Thumbelina ready for Violet's secret visit.

"Let's give you a makeover," said Makena.

"I'm glad we're friends," Thumbelina said, after Makena put pretty ribbons and sparkly barrettes in her hair.

Realizing that Thumbelina was a true friend, Makena knew she couldn't break her promise to keep the little Twillerbee a secret. Suddenly, the doorbell rang. It was Violet!

Makena quickly sent Violet away, but not before Thumbelina saw her and thought that Makena had broken her promise. Heartbroken, Thumbelina flew back home with Lola.

Makena raced to Twillerbee Field to apologize. "Thumbelina," she called. "I know now that *you* are my true friend, and I want to help you save your home."

"I believe you," Thumbelina said as she came out from hiding. "But we have to convince your parents to save Twillerbee Field—before it's too late!"

r friends
enhouse
amazed!

Thumbelina had a great idea. She and he
magically transformed Makena's empty gre
into a lush tearoom. Makena's parents were

They realized what Makena had been trying to tell them and promised to always make time for her. Makena's parents agreed to stop construction on the field—but the bulldozers were about to start the demolition!

Makena and her parents quickly drove toward Twillerbee Field, but they got caught in traffic. Jumping on her bike, Makena took Thumbelina and raced ahead to the site.

"Stop!" Makena shouted to the construction workers. Recognizing Makena, the crew stopped.

Twillerbee Field and the Twillerbabies were saved!

"We've got to protect this land and keep the Twillerbees a secret," said Makena to her parents. "But how?"

"I think I have an idea…," her dad replied.

225

Instead of building a skateboard factory, Makena and her parents turned the field into a beautiful nature preserve. The Twillerbees' home was now safe and sound and would remain secret. Makena and her parents always met Thumbelina and her friends there for tea—to talk, to listen, and to laugh.

Far away in a magical place called Flutterfield was a kingdom of butterfly fairies. The fairies didn't like when the sun went down because they were afraid of the hungry Skeezites who came out at night. Luckily, Queen Marabella had filled the trees with magical glowing flowers to protect the butterfly fairies. As long as Marabella lived, there would be light in Flutterfield.

One pretty fairy named Mariposa was different from all the other fairies. She liked the dark sky because she loved to study the stars. "Look," Mariposa said as she pointed out a constellation to her best friend, Willa. "There's the Archer's bow and arrow."

Mariposa and Willa worked for two bossy sisters named Rayna and Rayla.

"Mariposa, you have to beflutter all my gowns before the palace ball tonight," cried Rayna.

"And I need sparkly thistleburst for my hair," demanded Rayla. "The prince needs to see me shin

After helping the two sisters get ready, Mariposa and Willa flew off with them to the ball.

Willa was eager to go to the ball. But Mariposa didn't want to go inside because she didn't think she'd fit in. The queen's royal assistant, Henna, tried to convince her, but Mariposa felt more comfortable studying the stars and reading her book.

Mariposa thought Henna was a very kind fairy—but she wasn't! Henna was secretly plotting to take over Flutterfield and had poisoned the queen with an evil potion.

Mariposa flew around looking for a place to read—and bumped into Prince Carlos! The prince was impressed by Mariposa's knowledge of the stars and her interest in faraway places.

After the ball, Prince Carlos asked Mariposa for help. "The queen is very sick," said the prince. "Soon Flutterfield's lights will go out and we will all be in danger. Can you take this map and find the cure?"

Mariposa agreed, but she couldn't do it alone.

When Rayna and Rayla heard about Mariposa's special
mission, they volunteered to help so they could impress
the prince.

Soon Mariposa and the sisters had flown far beyond Flutterfield's protective lights—and Skeezites were everywhere! To make matters worse, Rayna had lost the map!

Remembering that they needed to go east to the Bewilderness, Mariposa followed the stars to find it. There they met a cute and playful creature named Zinzie.

Zinzie led the fairies to two mermaids who knew where the cure was.

But the mermaids were selfish and only agreed to help if they could get rare Conkle Shells in return.

Mariposa and the sisters dove into the water and quickly found the shells—but woke the Sea Beast! Luckily, the fairies worked together and swam in different directions to outsmart the monster.

"Fly with the arc of the sun and you will find the cure in the Cave of Reflection," the mermaids said as they swam off with the Conkle Shells.

241

After flying for hours, the fairies reached the Cave of Reflection. The tiny Fairy Speck told them that the cure was hidden behind a star in the sky.

"The Archer is a navigator in the sky," said Mariposa. "His arrow points to the correct star."

"Are you sure?" asked the Fairy Speck. "That star is all alone and is meaningless."

"Every star is there for a reason," said Mariposa. "They don't have to fit in to be important. They just have to be themselves."

When Mariposa chose the lone star, it transformed into the cure—and Mariposa's wings magically grew larger and more beautiful.

With the cure in hand, the friends rushed to save the queen!

Back at the palace, Henna took control of the kingdom with her horrible Skeezites. Prince Carlos tried to stop them, but there were too many.

Suddenly, Mariposa and her friends arrived.

"You've never felt like you belonged in Marabella's kingdom," Henna told Mariposa, trying to trick her. "But you will in mine. Everyone will love you."

"I'm happy with who I am," Mariposa declared as she flew to the queen's side with the cure. Queen Marabella awoke, and all of Flutterfield was bright again. The Skeezites screamed in pain and fled, along with the evil Henna.

"I'll be back!" she cried.

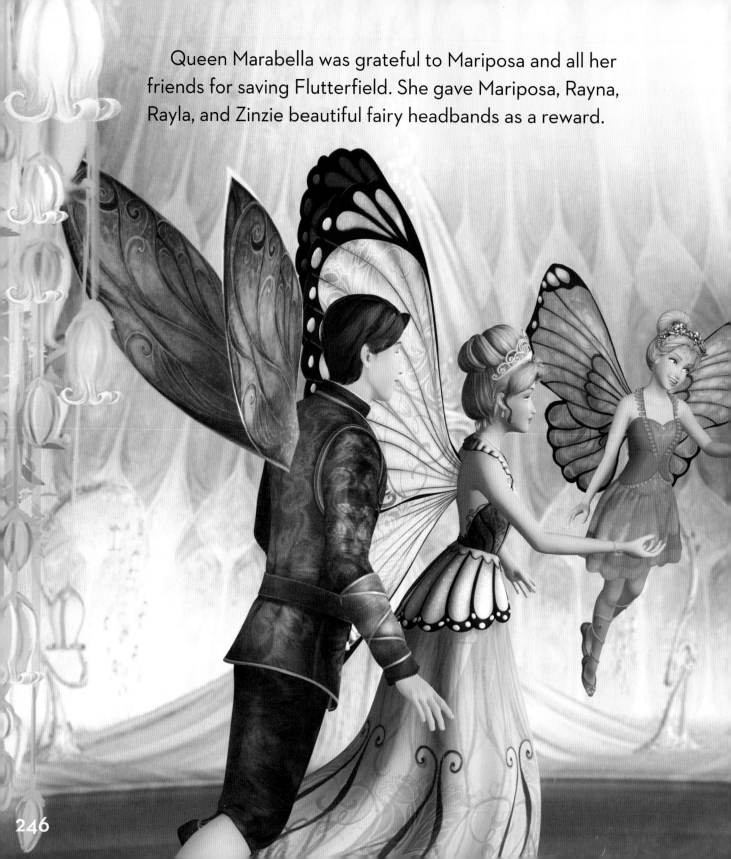

Queen Marabella was grateful to Mariposa and all her friends for saving Flutterfield. She gave Mariposa, Rayna, Rayla, and Zinzie beautiful fairy headbands as a reward.

Mariposa had never been so happy. She had made special new friends—and discovered just how special she was, too!

Once upon a time, there were two beautiful best friends who lived in a humble cottage in the woods. Alexa loved violets and was a little shy, while Liana loved roses and was very daring. The girls didn't have much, but they shared everything—especially their love of singing.

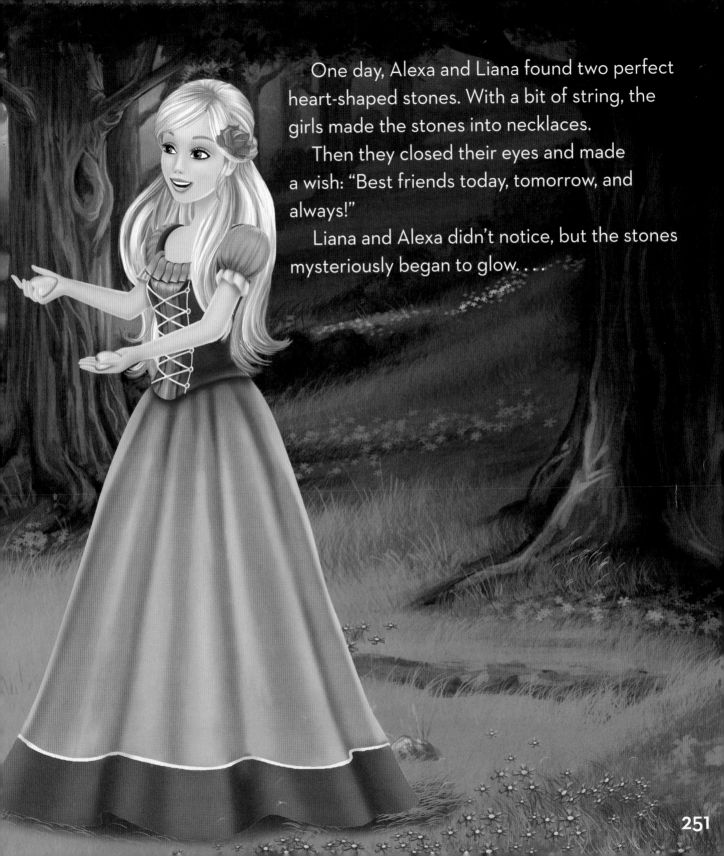

One day, Alexa and Liana found two perfect heart-shaped stones. With a bit of string, the girls made the stones into necklaces.

Then they closed their eyes and made a wish: "Best friends today, tomorrow, and always!"

Liana and Alexa didn't notice, but the stones mysteriously began to glow. . . .

Later that day, Alexa and Liana met an old woman near their cottage. She was very hungry, so the girls offered her something to eat. For their kindness, the old woman gave them a small antique mirror.

When they returned home, the friends started to sing their favorite song—and were amazed when a third voice joined them.

A young girl named Melody was hiding in the mirror!

Melody was from the birthplace of music, the Diamond Castle. She worked as an apprentice for the muses, or guardians of music.

The muses played beautifully, especially the flutist, Lydia.

"Dori, Phedra, and Lydia were all friends at first, but then Lydia became selfish and wanted everyone to do what she wanted," said Melody. "When they refused, she left and transformed her flute to play evil spells."

Lydia wanted to rule the Diamond Castle, so the other muses had used magic to hide it. Furious, Lydia had played her evil flute and turned the muses to stone.

Melody had escaped with the only key to the castle's hiding place, then hidden herself inside the mirror. And she had not uttered a sound—until she sang with Alexa and Liana.

Unfortunately, Lydia's helper, Slyder, heard Melody's singing and quickly alerted Lydia.

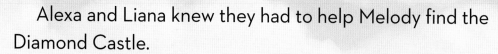

Alexa and Liana knew they had to help Melody find the Diamond Castle.

"It is hidden near the Seven Stones," Melody told them.

The girls quickly set off on their journey. Along the way, they met two adorable puppies that they named Lily and Sparkles.

As they traveled through a dark forest, Alexa, Liana, and Melody ran right into Lydia and Slyder.

"Give me the mirror," Lydia said, "and you can have all of these jewels."

But Alexa and Liana would never betray their friend. Furious, Lydia tried to turn them into stone with her flute—but the girls' necklaces magically protected them!

Alexa and Liana tried to run away, but Slyder flew after them. Luckily, two handsome twin musicians, Ian and Jeremy, helped the girls escape.

After thanking Ian and Jeremy for their kindness, Liana,
Alexa, Melody and the puppies traveled west toward the

As the girls reached a hilltop, they saw a beautiful manor.

"Welcome," said the butler. "This is all for you!"

Alexa, Liana, and Melody couldn't believe their eyes! There were tables full of food and closets full of beautiful gowns. It was everything they had ever wished for.

"But we can't stay," said Liana. "We need to help Melody find the Diamond Castle."

Tired and a little afraid, Alexa decided to stay at the manor.

Sadly, Liana left with Sparkles and Melody.

"I can't believe Liana chose Melody over me," Alexa said as she pulled off her necklace and threw it to the floor.

Just then, Lydia appeared. The manor was a trap! Without her necklace, Alexa fell under Lydia's wicked spell and revealed that the girls had gone to the Seven Stones.

Slyder quickly flew to the Seven Stones and brought Liana, Melody, and Sparkles to Lydia's secret lair.

"Melody, show me where the Diamond Castle is—or Alexa is doomed!"
Lydia demanded. To save her friend, Melody quickly agreed.

But as Lydia left with Melody, Slyder pushed Liana and Alexa into a
molten lava pit! Luckily, the girls landed on a narrow ledge. Then loyal Lily
brought Liana Alexa's missing necklace.

"Best friends today, tomorrow, and always," Liana said as she placed the
necklace back around her best friend's neck. Instantly, the spell was broken.

Liana and Alexa soon found Melody and Lydia in a misty glade.

"Come to me," Lydia commanded the girls as she played her evil flute. Liana and Alexa pretended to be under Lydia's spell and walked toward a churning whirlpool. But at the last moment, Liana grabbed Lydia's flute and threw it into the swirling waters.

Lydia dropped the mirror and lunged after her enchanted flute. "No!" she cried as she was pulled down into the whirlpool's gloomy depths.

With Lydia gone, Liana and Alexa used Melody's key to find the Diamond Castle—it was a special song! As the girls began to sing, the most beautiful castle, with shimmering diamonds, appeared before their eyes.

As they entered the jeweled
halls, Liana's and Alexa's dresses
magically transformed into
beautiful gowns.

Then sparkles of light circled
the mirror. Melody appeared
before them—she was finally free!

"Thank you!" Melody
exclaimed with happiness. The
three girls hugged each other
tightly.

Just then, Lydia angrily rode in
on Slyder's back and began to play
her evil flute. Thinking quickly,
the three girls started playing the
Diamond Castle's enchanted
instruments. They played and sang
in perfect harmony.

"No!" cried Lydia.

Melody, Liana, and Alexa's
beautiful music protected them
against the evil spell—and Lydia
and Slyder turned to stone!

All of Lydia's spells were broken, and soon the muses were no longer statues.

"For your bravery," the muses declared to Liana and Alexa, "we appoint you Princesses of Music."

270

Everyone cheered, and there was a grand celebration. "Best friends today, tomorrow, and always," Liana and Alexa said together.

The muses invited Liana and Alexa to live at the Diamond Castle, but the girls chose to return to their humble cottage instead. As they left the castle, Melody and the muses had one last gift for Liana and Alexa—a jeweled carriage!

As the girls rode home, they realized that their friendship was as rich and bright as a beautiful diamond.

Barbie *as*

The Island
Princess

Long ago, a beautiful young girl named Ro was shipwrecked on a tropical island. With no other humans on the island, Ro was raised by some friendly animals: Sagi, the red panda; Azul, the handsome peacock; and Tika, the sweet young elephant. Together they became a happy family.

Ro loved Sagi, Tika, and Azul very much, and each night she sang to them a lovely lullaby:

"It's magic when you are here beside me.
Close your eyes and let me hold you tight.
Everything that I could ever need is
Right here in my arms tonight."

One day, a handsome prince came to explore the island. He was amazed that the young woman could speak to animals!

"Where did you come from?" he asked.

"Sagi tells me I came from the sea a long time ago," answered the girl. "My name is Ro."

The prince was enchanted by Ro. "My name is Prince Antonio," he said. "Will you come back to the kingdom of Appolonia with me?"

Ro agreed—as long as she could bring her animal family along. During the journey, Ro and Antonio started to fall in love. And soon the prince dreamed of making Ro his princess.

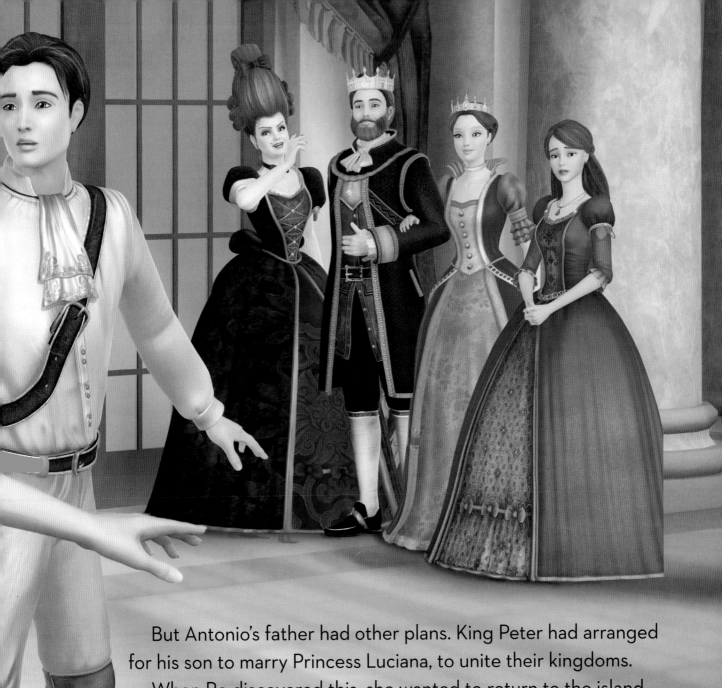

But Antonio's father had other plans. King Peter had arranged for his son to marry Princess Luciana, to unite their kingdoms.

When Ro discovered this, she wanted to return to the island. But the prince didn't love Luciana. He loved Ro and begged her to stay. Ro accepted his offer—but only if she could be with her animal family. So Ro, Sagi, Azul, and Tika all moved into the royal greenhouse. The island roses there reminded them of their home.

Queen Ariana desperately wanted her daughter, Luciana, to marry the prince—but for a different reason than King Peter. Long before, after failing to take over the kingdom, Queen Ariana and her family had been banished to a pig farm. Ever since, Ariana had vowed to get revenge. With her daughter married to the prince, Queen Ariana would finally overthrow King Peter and control his kingdom!

The prince wanted his parents to like Ro, so he arranged for them all to have tea. Unfortunately, Ro didn't know anything about tea parties. "Watch me," whispered Luciana as she picked up her teacup.

"Thank you," Ro whispered back. She was glad she had found a friend.

The next day, King Peter held an engagement ball for Prince Antonio and Princess Luciana—and everyone in the kingdom was invited. Ro had never been to a ball before. She was excited, but she didn't have anything to wear. Luckily, Queen Danielle's monkey, Tallulah, offered to help. She and Sagi, Tika, and Azul created a beautiful gown.

"You're going to have a great time at the ball," Tallulah said.

As soon as Ro entered the ballroom, the prince couldn't take his eyes off her. "May I have this dance?" he asked.

Queen Ariana was furious! She wanted to make sure that Princess Luciana married the prince. So Ariana commanded her pet rats to sprinkle a sleeping powder onto the food of all the animals in the kingdom. Then she would blame Ro and her animal friends for spreading the sleeping sickness.

When the animals mysteriously fell asleep, King
Peter believed that Ro and her animals were
responsible for the illness—and had them all thrown
into the dungeon!

Prince Antonio demanded that Ro be released,
but the king would agree only if Antonio married
Princess Luciana. Sadly, the prince accepted.

Ro and her animal friends were quickly put on a boat back to their island. Unfortunately, Azul had eaten some of the sleeping powder, too! Ro recognized that the powder was made from sunset herb. "We need the island roses from the greenhouse to save him," she said.

Suddenly, the friends were knocked overboard. As the waves crashed around them, Ro remembered being shipwrecked.

"Don't give up, Rosella!" her father had told her.

"My name is Rosella," she said in wonderment.

With newfound strength and hope, Ro called to the dolphins for help.

At the palace, the wedding of Prince Antonio and Princess Luciana was about to start.

Meanwhile, Ro arrived at the palace and sneaked into the greenhouse. Just as she finished making the antidote from island roses, Queen Ariana appeared.

"How dare you interrupt the wedding!" Ariana cried.

Just then, a tiny bird told Ro that Ariana had put sunset herb in the animals' food and on the wedding cake.

Realizing she was found out, Queen Ariana fled toward her carriage.

Ro quickly threw a pike at one of the carriage wheels, and the queen tumbled to the ground—and into a pigsty!

Back at the palace, Ro quickly gave the antidote to all the animals, and they slowly awoke.

King Peter approached Ro. "I'm sorry I misjudged you," he said.

"Will you marry me?" Prince Antonio asked Ro.

With Princess Luciana's blessing, Ro agreed. "But please call me Rosella. That's my real name."

Just then, a wedding guest who had overheard came to them. "I had a daughter named Rosella," Queen Marissa said. "But she was lost at sea."

Ro started to softly sing her favorite lullaby:

"It's magic when you are here beside me.
Close your eyes and let me hold you tight. . . ."

". . . Everything that I could ever need is right here in my arms tonight," Queen Marissa finished.

"Mother!" Ro cried.

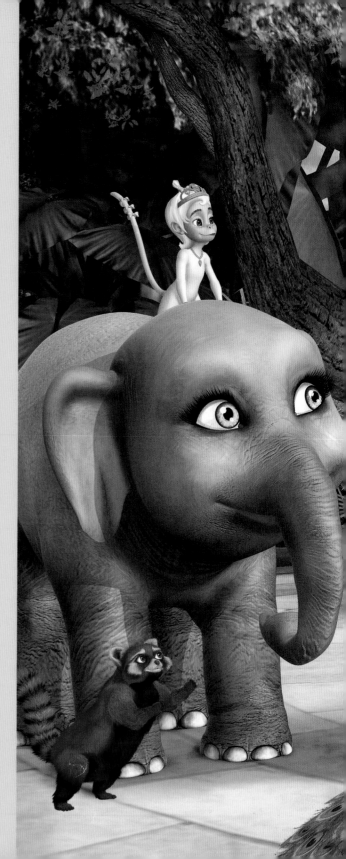

Soon the wedding of Prince Antonio and Princess
Rosella was held at the palace.

Prince Antonio married his island princess, and
they lived happily ever after—with all their family
beside them!

Barbie
in the
12
Dancing
RINCESSES

Once upon a time, there was a kind king who had twelve beautiful daughters. The king raised the princesses as best he could, but he needed help.

"I love them," the king said to himself. "But at times I don't understand them."

Each of the princesses had a different hobby, but they *all* loved one thing . . .

. . . dancing! Princess Genevieve especially loved to dance. Every day she and her sisters would practice their leaps and twirls in the palace garden. The royal cobbler, Derek, would often bring the princesses new dancing shoes and mend their old ones. Derek was secretly in love with Princess Genevieve.

Knowing that the raising of his daughters called for a woman's touch, the king asked his cousin, Duchess Rowena, to come live in the castle. Rowena wanted to be queen, so she plotted to slowly poison the king. But first she had to pretend to help with the girls' upbringing.

"You must learn to be proper princesses," Rowena declared as she took away their beautiful gowns and playthings—and even forbade them to dance!

The triplets were especially upset because it was their birthday. "We always danced on our birthdays when Mother was alive," Lacey complained.

To cheer them up, the other princesses gave each of the triplets a copy of their mother's favorite book, *The Dancing Princess.* "She had one made for each of us with our favorite flower on the cover," explained Ashlyn.

Everyone listened quietly as Genevieve read the story about a princess who danced on special stones, revealing a hidden magical world.

Suddenly, Lacey stumbled and her book landed on a stone with the same flower painted on it!

"It's just like in Mother's story!" exclaimed Courtney. The sisters quickly matched their books to the different stones.

"In the story, the princess danced on the stones to find the magical world," Genevieve added. As the princesses gracefully danced from stone to stone, a bell chimed. On the last stone, Genevieve twirled three times. Suddenly, the stone sank down, revealing a set of stairs leading to . . .

. . . the most beautiful place they had ever seen! Silver trees and jeweled flowers surrounded a golden pavilion with musical instruments.

"I wish there was music," Genevieve whispered. With those words, a diamond flower sprinkled magic dust on the instruments—and they began to play! The princesses leaped and twirled to the music.

"Ouch!" Lacey exclaimed as she tripped and scraped her knee. "Why can't I be good at something?"

"Mother always told us, big or small, there's a difference only you can make," Genevieve gently told her sister. She dipped her handkerchief in the sparkling lake and dabbed her little sister's knee. Amazingly, the scrape disappeared!

The sisters danced well into the night before they returned to their bedroom. And the next morning, all twelve princesses were so tired that they couldn't stay awake! Rowena was getting very suspicious by the time Derek arrived to fix their shoes.

"It looks like someone's been having a good time," Derek said as he polished and mended the princesses' worn shoes.

"We did," Genevieve said as she danced the steps from the night before. "But I don't trust Rowena. Will you find out what she's up to?"

"I'll do my best," the cobbler promised.

Meanwhile, Rowena was convinced that the princesses had sneaked out and danced all night with princes. So that evening, the duchess ordered her henchman, Desmond, to guard the princesses' bedroom door and make sure they didn't leave. But as soon as he fell asleep, Genevieve and her sisters sneaked back to the golden pavilion.

The girls laughed and danced with beautiful paper fans until the soles of their shoes were worn through again.

Soon Derek discovered Rowena's plot to become queen. He rushed to the princesses' bedroom to tell Genevieve, but they were all missing. Remembering Genevieve's dance steps, Derek stepped on the stones—and found Genevieve in the enchanted world!

But Rowena had secretly followed Derek to the magic pavilion. There she came up with a wicked plan. She picked two of the enchanted flowers and returned to the princesses' bedroom. Then Rowena smashed all the magic stones. The princesses were trapped in the golden pavilion!

"I wish to know the way out," Genevieve said. Instantly, the jeweled flowers sprinkled magic dust on special stones.

"May I have this dance?" Derek asked. As Genevieve and Derek danced across the stones together, a staircase appeared for their escape!

Derek and the princesses rushed to the palace. Realizing she was cornered, Rowena held up one of the magic flowers. "I wish for armor to protect the queen," she said. Instantly, a suit of armor came to life! Thinking quickly, Derek grabbed the fireplace poker and smashed the armor to pieces.

"I wish you would dance your life away," Rowena shouted, using her last enchanted flower. Magic dust blew toward Genevieve and Derek, but Genevieve quickly flipped open her paper fan and blew the dust right back toward the duchess. "Help! Help!" Rowena cried as her feet danced her far away from the castle.

With Rowena finally gone, the sisters had to save their father. The poison had begun to work and the king was very ill.

"I think I can help," Lacey said. She gave her father some water from her vial. "It's from the lake. I took some after I scraped my knee."

Slowly, the king's eyes fluttered open and he smiled at his daughters.

"It worked!" Genevieve exclaimed.

"Where would I be without you?" the king asked his littlest daughter. "Your mother always told me . . ."

"Big or small, there's a difference only you can make," finished Lacey with a smile.

"And you all have made a difference," the king said to his daughters.

That spring, a beautiful wedding took place at the palace.
Everyone came to celebrate the marriage of Derek and
Princess Genevieve—and they all danced the night away.